ONE SWEET CHRISTMAS

ONE SWEET CHRISTMAS

MARIE LONG

ONE
SWEET
CHRISTMAS

ONE SWEET CHRISTMAS

CHAPTER 1

SWEET PEACH BAKE SHOP WAS SLAMMED tonight. Resident pastry chef Arianna Willis was debuting her Christmas Memories pairing of peppermint cookies and white hot chocolate during the weeklong Festival of Lights leading up to Christmas Day, and a record crowd had gathered. The line of bundled patrons was out the door of the tiny shop, wrapped around the corner, and down the sidewalk of White Pine's historic downtown. Arianna scrambled behind the counter, preparing drinks, packaging cookies, and ringing up customers. She had spent all morning baking, decorating, and preparing her limited-edition cookies and hot drink, expecting a small crowd for her soft launch. But she was selling her new offerings faster than she could blink.

After moving to the quaint Vermont town three years ago and acquiring the shop, Arianna had grown accustomed to the small crowds of locals and the few tourists who passed through during the year. But this holiday season was proving different. Christmas was a big deal in White Pine, and Arianna had never seen another town transform into such a magical storybook fantasy. As a result, the town had seen a larger influx of tourism than in past years.

Arianna was down to her last batch of cookies, and the line of waiting patrons didn't let up. She was sure to run out of treats well before six o'clock, when the festival's third evening of events began. Tonight was the snowman-building contest, and most of the patrons were families with small children. Arianna hated the thought of disappointing so many of them when she was unable to provide some sweet and delicious Christmas magic.

"I'd like one order of your Christmas Memories pairing," a man said in a smooth voice. "And can you package the cookie in a pretty box?"

Arianna shook off her thoughts. A tall man with almond-toned skin stood at the front of the line, bundled up in a black leather jacket and a black-and-grey plaid scarf. A warm smile traced his solid jawline, which sported a shadow of a beard. Her heart stuttered briefly, and she returned his contagious smile. "Coming right up, sir." She opened the glass display case and retrieved a Christmas tree–shaped peppermint cookie—the very last one—with a pair of metal tongs. She set the cookie in a small, wax paper–lined box printed with holly and candy cane images and secured the box with a glittering gold ribbon. *A sweet gift for his wife or child. What a thoughtful, loving gentleman.*

Turning her back to him, she faced the hot chocolate machine and tried to focus while she filled a paper cup with white hot chocolate. Her brain was frazzled. She wondered if that mysterious, handsome gentleman was local or just passing through. She'd never seen him before. Still, the man's presence made her heart stutter, an emotion she hadn't felt in years. She couldn't worry about relationships and how long it had been since she'd had a date when she had a business to run. And with Christmas approaching in three days, all her efforts would be spent baking and helping others make sweet memories.

She set the cup and box on the counter. As she rang up the items, the man slid some money across to her.

"Keep the change," he said.

Furrowing her brow, Arianna looked from the register to his hand splayed over a twenty-dollar bill. Her eyes widened slightly. She wasn't sure whether she should be surprised by his generous tip or by the fact that he didn't sport a ring. *Must be a gift for his girlfriend, then.* Arianna hoped that girl knew just how lucky she was to have a handsome gentleman like him. "Th-thank you," Arianna finally said.

The man grinned and took the items. "You're welcome"—he glanced at her name tag— "Arianna?"

She smiled softly and nodded. Hearing her name on his tongue brought warmth and joy to her heart.

"Nice to meet you. I'm Mark." His eyes bounced back to the display case and suddenly widened. "Wait, are those macarons?"

Arianna held her head proudly. Those were her prized sweets. After many failures, she'd managed to master the art of making the perfect macaron. "Sure are."

"Not many chefs can pull off the perfect macaron. Yours are flawless. Smooth skin with just the right lift in the feet. You have a good folding technique since the shells have a healthy rise. I've never seen anything more amazing."

Arianna beamed and felt her cheeks flaming. He sounded knowledgeable. *Is he a chef himself, perhaps?* "Thank you."

He nodded and turned as if to leave. "Thanks for the chat. I'll leave you to it. Merry Christmas."

She watched him squeeze through the crowd at the entrance and disappear into the square under the gentle haze of falling snow. *Merry Christmas, Mark.*

Chapter 2

DID YOU GET WHAT I ASKED?"

Mark regarded the young woman who sat among several stacks of books beneath her vendor tent in the main square. Her thin lips rose in an amused smile. Mark scratched the back of his head. He couldn't stop thinking about that gorgeous pastry chef at Sweet Peach Bake Shop. After getting over a bad relationship two months ago, he never thought he would be interested in finding love again. But somehow, that brief encounter with Arianna had ignited a new spark of possibility. Mustering the courage to talk to her, however, would be a challenge. She appeared so busy in her shop, he figured she wouldn't have time for him. But he had to try to connect with her, at least. He was vacationing in White Pine for only a week before he headed to Las Vegas. "Yeah, Raina," he finally said, handing the woman the cup of white hot chocolate and the decorative cookie box. "And I apparently got the very last ones."

Raina's eyes glittered as she took the items and peeked inside the box. "Oh, how lucky! Thanks."

Mark looked at her expectantly. "Well? Are you going to give it to me now or what?"

She took a long sip of chocolate and smiled in satisfaction. "Mmm. Yes, yes, I know. A deal's a deal." She reached behind her and retrieved a thick book off a stack. "And a trade for a trade. Hope you'll find better use for this than the last owner."

"Thanks." Mark took the book and stared at the hard cover. He ran his fingers over the raised lettering that read *Vintage Christmas Recipes of Yesteryear*. The book had caught his eye when he'd paid a visit to the town square earlier that afternoon to check out the festivities. An avid collector of cookbooks, and a sucker for vintage recipes, Mark believed this book in particular would help him hone his culinary skills. He needed the perfect recipe to present when he flew to Las Vegas and appeared live on stage with his favorite celebrity chef, Justina Ayers. All his dreams had come true when he'd been selected as one of the ten winners of Justina's Top Chef contest. Mark had received a letter from Justina's manager letting him know that he would appear on the daytime television show *Cooking with Justina* next week. By impressing his longtime celebrity idol, Mark could validate himself and get the exposure that might result in an offer of being a head chef at some fancy restaurant—or having a television show of his own.

Clutching the book under his arm, he left the square. On his way to the bed-and-breakfast where he was staying, he passed by the sweet shop and noticed a sign on the door that read, "Out of the Christmas Memories pairing. Sorry for the inconvenience!" The massive line of people that had been wrapped around the block had been reduced to a few patrons lingering inside. Arianna was still hard at work fulfilling orders, her bronze skin covered in a thin sheen of sweat. Her dark-brown eyes bounced from the register, to the patrons, then to the food as she scrambled about. Mark hesitated before entering her shop, wondering if she would bother talking to him.

If he was going to approach her again, it might as well be while the place wasn't busy. His time was running out, so he headed across the street. As he reached the entrance, the last patron left, and the owner was finally alone. Mark dusted his jacket of the tiny flakes of snow and ducked inside. Arianna was behind the counter, transferring empty trays from the display cases to a large dishwashing sink. It was still a few hours from closing time, and her shop was already devoid of her sweet stock.

With her head down, Arianna energetically spritzed the countertop with pine-scented spray and wiped it down with a holly-printed cloth. Mark approached the counter, and she stopped and looked up as if doing a double take. "Oh, h-hi again. Back for more? I'm very sorry about this, but I'm completely sold out of everything."

Mark smiled. "It's a good problem to have, though."

She briefly matched his smile before the corners of her mouth slowly dropped. "Yes, I suppose it is. I just always feel horrible to see all the disappointed faces of families and children who were unable to get any Christmas pastries or hot chocolate."

He frowned as well. "Sounds like you need help making more stock."

"That would be great, but I don't know any experienced pastry chefs around here."

Mark's frown lifted, and he regarded her, amused. "I'm no stranger to working in pastry kitchens. They were some of my most memorable jobs."

Tilting her head to the side, Arianna narrowed her eyes slightly and scrunched her nose. "I'm sorry. Who are you, again?"

He released an airy chuckle. "I'm Mark, remember? Mark Ellison. I'm just vacationing here for the week of Christmas, then I will be off to an… interview for a chef position." He was careful not to mention Justina's name, as he wasn't sure whether dropping a celebrity's name might ultimately backfire on him.

Arianna blinked once. "Wait. So you *are* a chef!"

"I'd like to think I am. I've been exposed to a wide variety of cuisines, having interned at cafés and restaurants back in New York City and Long Island, my current home."

"You like working as a chef?"

"What chef doesn't like being able to explore their passion of creating unique dishes that wow customers?"

One corner of her lips tugged upward. "There's a place in town called Frandles Gourmet Cuisine, which is owned by a locally famous chef. While I've never been there, I've heard nothing but glowing reviews about the place. I heard they're looking for a sous chef."

Mark was slightly taken aback by her response. Frandles sounded like the kind of white-tablecloth restaurant where people went on dates. The fact that she'd never been there might have meant she didn't have a date. Could a gorgeous, hardworking woman like her really be single? "How about we go there tonight? I'll get us the best seats in the house."

A hint of red tinted her cheeks. "That sounds nice, but honestly? I'd prefer a quiet meal at home."

Simple and honest. There was a certain charming appeal about that. "I hear you. Okay, then. How about I invite you for a nice home-cooked meal at the bed-and-breakfast I'm staying at?"

The redness on her cheeks became more prominent. "You're persistent, aren't you?"

"Well, you said you can't find any experienced chefs to help you around here, so maybe I can volunteer my time at your shop for a bit."

She blinked. "You want to work for me?"

"Sure. Why not? I don't mind. Come to the bed-and-breakfast tonight, and I'll prove my culinary skills." He cracked a smile.

"You work as a chef at a bed-and-breakfast?"

"I'm not exactly an employee there. I've been volunteering my time since I arrived four days ago. I helped Paulette, the owner, make some quiche for breakfast one morning, and she was so impressed with my cooking, she pretty much lets me use the kitchen anytime."

She raised her eyebrows. "Wow, you must be pretty good."

He shook his head. "I'm just a man who loves to cook. That's all." *Especially for a gorgeous, charming woman like you.*

"All right, then. I guess I'll take you up on your offer." She sighed. "This is the first time I've had to close up shop early because I sold out of everything."

"Be ready for the rush again tomorrow."

She made a face. "I wish this hadn't happened during the week of Christmas, when I've had to turn so many children and families away. I called my pairing Christmas Memories for a reason."

He understood and appreciated her treats being in high demand. That was why he had to make tonight's dinner extra special. He gave her the address of the bed-and-breakfast. "Come by around eight tonight."

Her eyebrows rose slightly. "They actually serve dinner at that bed-and-breakfast?"

"Why not?"

"Seems odd."

He laughed. "Okay. No, they don't serve dinner there. But they have a full kitchen with a stove. Why couldn't they serve whatever they wanted? Besides, I'm allowed to use the kitchen whenever I want."

She chewed her bottom lip. "Are you sure you'll have enough time to cook dinner?"

Her continuous excuses amused him and only solidified the fact that he had one chance to make the night special. "Two hours is plenty of time." He backed toward the door. "It's a date, then. Right?"

She watched him a moment, the confused expression on her face softening. "It's a date. See you at eight."

CHAPTER 3

A DATE. MARK NEVER THOUGHT HE WOULD
actually say those words again. And he couldn't
believe Arianna had accepted his offer. What a
vacation this was turning out to be. He hadn't
thought relationships would ever be in the cards for
him again. After frequently coming home at late
hours as a result of working overtime as a fill-in or
assistant chef, he'd broken up with his girlfriend of
seven months. His skills were in high demand, and
he'd never refused to help a young upstart who was
interested in the culinary arts. But his culinary
passion had put a toll on his relationship, and he

figured it was best to never get involved again, to never break another heart.

He'd come to White Pine to escape the stresses of his break-up, his layoff from his relief-chef job at an exclusive five-star restaurant in Manhattan, and the fact that he would be spending Christmas alone this year. A holiday trip to a cozy bed-and-breakfast was just what he needed to remind him of the memorable Christmases he'd spent with his family as a boy. Once Christmas was over, he would be off to Las Vegas to meet Justina Ayers.

Clutching his newly acquired cookbook under one arm, Mark strode down the snow-covered sidewalk, admiring the lighted houses and yard decorations in the neighborhood just a few blocks away from the square. People bundled up in coats and scarves admired some of the brightly lit houses that twinkled with carnival colors. Mark quietly brushed past the oglers and made his way to the pastel-pink colonial-style cottage of White Pine Bed & Breakfast. He opened the gate to the waist-high white picket fence that wrapped around the property, and he climbed a set of brick stairs leading to the front porch. Multicolored Christmas lights strung along the eaves and frame of the front door twinkled in unique patterns. A large pine wreath decorated with tiny white lights, pinecones, and colorful orbs hung prominently on the door's glass window.

Entering, Mark was greeted with the homey warmth of the small fire from the common room fireplace. Paulette, the manager and innkeeper, sat on a padded stool before a group of children sitting cross-legged on the floor, and their parents were seated on the couches and chairs around the room. Paulette read Christmas stories from a large hardback picture book, and the children watched, clearly intrigued, holding little paper cups of hot chocolate topped with small marshmallows.

Mark stopped at the narrow doorway to the common room and watched Paulette's rendition of *'Twas the Night Before Christmas* come to life with distinctive expressions and intonations from her aged face. Though almost eighty, Paulette was still as spry as ever. She met Mark's gaze with a brief nod then returned to the story.

Leaning against the doorframe, Mark crossed his arms and smiled. He was reminded of his childhood, when he and his sisters had gathered around their father, who told them popular Christmas stories in his perfect Santa Claus impersonation.

"But I heard him exclaim, ere he drove out of sight..." Paulette grinned at the children. "Ready? Let's say it together."

Mark stayed silent and watched as the children straightened, their faces glowing with anticipation. Then they and their parents joined Paulette and recited, *"Happy Christmas to all, and to all a good night!"*

"The end." Paulette closed the book, and everyone applauded. The parents gathered their children and left the room.

Mark pushed off the doorframe and approached Paulette. "You had quite the audience tonight."

"Seeing all those happy kids' faces is why I love my job." Paulette returned the storybook to a shelf behind the couch. "What can I do for you?"

"I was wondering if I can use two of those green bell peppers you have in the fridge."

Her eyebrows shot up. "Of course. That kitchen is yours. Just be mindful that we do have other guests here."

He nodded. "Absolutely. I intend to make some dinner."

"We don't serve dinner here."

"I know, but…" He rubbed the back of his head. "I, uh, met someone today, and she—"

"Stop right there." Paulette grinned from ear to ear. "Oh, my goodness. You've only been here a few days, and you've already found love. Who's the lucky lady?"

His heart thrummed with excitement as he told Paulette about his encounter with Arianna.

Paulette's face softened. "How wonderful. You've been such a godsend, helping us in the kitchen and making such an amazing breakfast, and now you want to surprise that lovely young lady with a home-cooked meal. I certainly can't say no to that. She is a dear, that Arianna. But she's such a workaholic. You're a gentleman to want to give her the break she so desperately needs."

He let out a relieved sigh. "Thanks for understanding."

"No, thank you! As if this day couldn't get any better, Christmas is in the air, and so is love." She shooed him off. "Well? What are you waiting for? Get to work, already! You don't have much time. You can use the Christmas china in the upper left cabinet, too."

Without another word, Mark rushed to the large kitchen, which, unlike the rest of the vintage-era house, was furnished with modern steel appliances. It wasn't nearly as big as the kitchens he was used to, but it had all of the equipment he needed.

He decided to put his skills to the test by creating a festive dish that was new to him, hoping to impress Arianna on the first try. Only then would he be convinced that he truly had what it took to turn any ingredient into a delectable meal. He placed the recipe book on the counter and flipped through its yellowed pages until he discovered the perfect meal to prepare with the available ingredients: stuffed pimientos, baked spiced ham slices, mashed potatoes, and cranberry sponge pudding. With only an hour and a half to spare, Mark got to work, preparing each dish in record time and using both ovens and stove tops. While everything baked and simmered, Mark found the Christmas-themed china plates and glasses and arranged them in the breakfast nook.

"What has our resident celebrity chef cooked up this time?" Paulette sniffed the air as she entered the kitchen. She wore a long green housedress, a pair of reading glasses resting atop her short white hair.

Mark drew his gaze from one of the ovens containing the pimientos and looked at the smiling innkeeper. "That was just breakfast. I'm no celebrity."

"You're just being modest. Breakfast or not, no one around here can do what you do in so little time."

He half smiled. The title of celebrity chef had a nice ring to it. Maybe after his guest appearance in Vegas, he just might earn it.

The front door creaked open, and someone walked in. Paulette craned her neck, and her face brightened. "Oh, that must be her now," she whispered to Mark then hurried out of the kitchen.

Mark prepared the dishes with pimientos, ham slices, and mashed potatoes, added a decorative garnish of rosemary and parsley, then covered the plates with metal cloches. He set the plates on the table and half filled two glasses with merlot. He stood back and took one last look at the table setting, ensuring everything was in its place, then he waited.

"Here, dear. Let me take your coat," Paulette said from the common room. Moments later, she and Arianna entered the breakfast nook.

Arianna glanced at Mark and stopped. Paulette quietly tiptoed away, giving Mark an encouraging thumbs-up.

It seemed Arianna had come straight from work. Her name tag was affixed to her black button-down blouse, and her candy cane–printed skirt had a dab of white flour in the same spot he'd remembered seeing when he was at her shop earlier.

She smiled apologetically, confirming his suspicions. "I'm sorry. I didn't get a chance to change. I hope I'm not underdressed."

"You're dressed perfectly." Mark gestured to an empty chair. "I'm glad you made it."

She stared intriguingly at the table spread. A small crease appeared at her brow. "It's just us?"

Mark laughed. "Of course it is. You thought there would be others?"

"There are other guests staying here, aren't there?"

"Yes, but this is a special dinner just for us." He patted the back of the chair.

Arianna's lips twisted into a coy smile, then she sat. Mark lifted the cloche from her plate, and a billow of steam escaped. She stared at her plate in apparent awe. "Wow, this looks and smells delicious. You actually made all this?"

"Yes, I did," he replied, sitting across from her and uncovering his plate.

She picked up her fork, and her smile grew coyer. "Were you really serious about wanting to work at my shop?"

"Yes. You've got a great thing going on there. I may not be in town for long, but I'd like to help you make more families happy for the holidays."

"How long are you here?"

He hated to be reminded that his stay was temporary and that soon, he might never see Arianna again. "Until the day after Christmas. Then I'm off to Vegas." He paused and bit his lip. *Maybe it won't hurt to tell her. I feel like I can trust her.* "Can you keep a secret?"

She nodded.

He took a deep breath then told her about his television appearance.

Arianna's face lit up. "Wow, I'm a huge fan of Justina's show. And you're going to be on it? That's amazing!"

"Yeah, I'm excited." But part of him was already starting to have mixed feelings about the show.

They enjoyed the main course while chatting about the town's upcoming events, including the Christmas dessert contest, which happened on Christmas Eve.

"You're going to enter, right?" Mark asked.

She stared at her empty plate and shrugged. "I don't know. I might be too busy at the shop to enter."

"We'll have to make sure that doesn't happen." Mark got up and retrieved the two small plates of cranberry sponge pudding from the refrigerator and served Arianna before putting down his own plate. He coupled the dessert with a glass of orange muscat wine.

"What a unique-looking dessert." Arianna took a small bite of the pudding. Her face suddenly lit up. "Wow, so tasty!"

"It's cranberry sponge pudding," Mark explained. "It's a vintage Christmas dessert recipe from the early twentieth century. I've always been a fan of classic Christmas recipes."

"It tastes like something my grandma would've made. And she was such an amazing cook."

Mark nodded. "Mine, too. I guess it's one of the reasons I enjoy making older recipes. They made some tasty desserts back then."

Arianna finished her dessert then sipped her wine. "Thank you for all this. I've never had a finer meal."

Mark chuckled. "So, does that mean I passed your test?"

She gave him a dubious look. "There was never a test, but I did enjoy this. And I'd be more than happy to have you volunteer your time."

Mark silently celebrated. At last, he would be able to work beside the amazing woman who was beginning to capture his heart. "Thanks for giving me a chance."

Her face softened. "No, thank you. The Christmas parade is tomorrow night, and I'm anticipating getting slammed again, so I'll be at it extra early in the morning."

He nodded. "Sounds good. I promise to be there bright and early."

She scooted her chair back and stood. "I should head home. Thank you for the wonderful dinner."

Mark got up as well. "I'll walk you home. It's late." He suddenly glimpsed Paulette shuffling into the next room. She caught his eye, and a wide smile parted her lips.

"Oh, goodness," Paulette said, coming in. "Leaving already?" She looked at Arianna innocently. "I do hope you enjoyed your visit, young lady."

Arianna grinned. "I did. Thank you for your hospitality. This bed-and-breakfast is so homey and cozy. I love how you've decorated for the holidays."

"Of course, dear. No one does Christmas better than I do." Paulette winked.

Mark raised his eyebrows at the older woman, who began clearing the table. *Impeccable timing. I wonder if she was eavesdropping all this time.*

Paulette paused from her work and placed her hand on Mark's shoulder. "Why don't you be a gentleman and walk this nice lady home, hmm?" She winked at him.

Warmth spread across Mark's face. He looked over at Arianna, who smiled back, a hint of amusement in her dark-brown eyes.

They walked down the sidewalk and farther into the small neighborhood, passing more houses decorated as if there were a competition for the brightest, most extravagant house. Arianna walked beside him with her hands shoved in her coat pockets. He wished he could hold her hand as they walked, but she still seemed unsure of him. That was understandable. One dinner date might not have been enough to convince her, but he wasn't going to give up.

"Isn't it beautiful?" Arianna asked wistfully, nodding toward a yard covered in multicolored lights. Their glow bounced off the blanket of snow like colorful twinkling stars. "This must be the brightest street in the neighborhood."

Mark glanced at the house, impressed with the workmanship, but his eyes couldn't help drifting to her profile. Wisps of her thick, curly hair poked out from beneath her knitted hat and caught snowflakes. The glow of the lights dancing off her bronze skin accented her serene beauty.

They turned down another block and walked to the end of the street to a small blue colonial-style home—the only one of the surrounding houses that wasn't decorated.

"I figured this was your house," he joked.

She let out an airy laugh. "How did you know?"

"Because I can already tell you're a hardworking pastry chef, and you probably have never given yourself a long-enough break to decorate your house."

"You guessed right. House decorating takes time, which I don't have after coming home from an exhausting workday."

He stood at the bottom of the stairs and watched her walk up the stoop. "Did you at least put up a Christmas tree?"

She turned and shook her head, pursing her lips. She took her hands out of her pockets, one of them holding her house key.

He eyed her free hand before staring at her face. Then he slowly ascended the stairs. "Maybe I can help you decorate sometime."

She turned her head away as he joined her at the top of the stoop. "Who knows when that will happen."

He studied her hand again then slowly took it. "Whenever you want."

Her gaze bounced back to him then down at their clasped hands. He gave her a small, reassuring squeeze. Mark could sense the wheels turning in her mind. Even beneath her gloves, he could feel the gentle warmth of her hand. She was clearly still unsure about him, but he wouldn't give up.

Finally, with a faint smile, Arianna slipped her hand out of his and turned to the door. "Thank you again for dinner and the nice walk. I'll see you bright and early tomorrow."

His heart stung with a slight feeling of disappointment. He stood back and watched her go inside. "Anytime. I promise to be there early. Have a good night."

She closed the door behind her, and Mark stood there for several moments, staring at the door, wondering if a relationship could ever be possible for the two of them.

Chapter 4

EARLY THE NEXT MORNING, AS ARIANNA walked through the square, she overheard Raina, the local bookseller, telling an elderly couple about "that celebrity chef" staying at the bed-and-breakfast. It must've really been a slow news day in town when that was all that was being drummed up. Arianna couldn't deny that Mark was an excellent chef—last night's dinner had been absolute perfection. But Mark also seemed to be just a normal guy on vacation. She couldn't get attached to him when his stay was temporary. She'd convinced herself of that when he'd walked her home. While it was a sweet gesture, and she was grateful, she was finished with experiencing heartbreak. She was determined to push from her mind that fateful day three years ago when she'd found out her boyfriend and college sweetheart was cheating on her. He'd stretched himself thin with obligations, so she'd figured he was just a kind man with a big heart. Her naivete had caused her pain, and she escaped far away from her ex and discovered this quaint, peaceful town of White Pine, which she'd since called home.

Today was the Christmas parade, which meant the town square would be extra busy. Arianna planned to make triple the amount of her treats. She didn't want a repeat of yesterday.

Not waiting on Mark to arrive, Arianna got to work. During the holidays, her shop opened at noon, which gave her ample time to prepare. But she wasn't sure if five hours would be nearly enough time for her to make so many batches. While the ovens heated, she constructed the pastries from doughs she'd prepared the previous night. Dozens of cake, cookie, and cupcake pans sat on the counter, ready to be filled with her sweet masterpieces.

An hour passed. She'd finished preparing six batches of sweets and glanced toward the door, catching a glimpse of bundled-up passersby. Still no sign of Mark. She frowned. She didn't want to believe he'd forgotten already. Perhaps he'd simply overslept. She averted her thoughts and cut her gaze to the rest of her shop's interior. She'd been so caught up with her work, she'd neglected to put up the Christmas decorations, save for a lone small paper Christmas tree sitting on the front counter.

A muffled rap came from the snow-powdered glass of the entrance door. Arianna perked. *Mark?* Then a pair of bright-red mittens pressed against the glass. A young woman's smiling face peered inside.

Arianna deflated at the sight of her friend Jamie, this year's event coordinator for the town's holiday festivities. Arianna had hoped the "Sorry, we're closed" sign would give her friend a hint to not disturb her while she worked. Although she would love to chat some other time, every second mattered—today more than ever. Arianna maneuvered around the front counter and unlocked the door.

Jamie, who was bundled up like an Eskimo, a bright-red scarf wrapped around her neck, shook off the excess powdery snowflakes from her light-blond hair and stepped inside. "Hey, girl." She locked the door behind her. "All ready to sell out again tonight?"

Arianna shook her head and returned behind the counter, where she transferred a batch of white chocolate macadamia cookies to one of the ovens. "As ready as I'll ever be."

Jamie looked around and tsked. "Geez, you haven't even decorated the place."

"Sure I did." Arianna filled the racks of the second oven with peppermint-chocolate cupcakes.

Jamie approached the front counter and picked up the flimsy paper Christmas tree. "You call this decorating?"

Arianna rolled her eyes, experiencing déjà vu over the same talk she and Mark had had last night. "I'd love to go all out with decorations, but there's only so many hours in a day, and I have things to bake and customers to serve."

"You need to take a break."

Arianna blew a raspberry. "If I don't get all this work done, I won't have a shop to decorate."

"Okay, then. Let me decorate this place for you."

"Thanks, but you don't have to do that. Besides, don't you have to help the committee with the parade stuff?"

"Yes, but I always have time to help a friend. Especially when it involves decorating for the holidays. C'mon. Let me do it. You won't even know I'm here."

Arianna gave her a dismissive wave then began cracking eggs into a large bowl. "I appreciate it, but I'll do it eventually."

Jamie rolled her eyes. "That pretty much means never. Christmas is in two days. You deserve a break, y'know. Or at least hire some help. You think I do all this event organizing alone? Heck no! It's a team effort."

Arianna half smiled at her friend's insistence. She couldn't remember the last time she'd taken a vacation or simply put her feet up for a day. Work was always on her mind, like during the dinner date she'd had with Mark, as divine as it had been. She hoped it wouldn't be their last date. "You'll be glad to know that I've hired some temporary help."

Jamie perked up, her bright-blue eyes widening. "Really? That's great! Are they here now? When are they starting?" She craned her neck, attempting to peer toward the back of the kitchen.

Arianna shrugged. "I'm not sure where he is. I guess he slept in. Or maybe he changed his mind." She chewed her bottom lip. Had he truly forgotten? Or was he deliberately standing her up? Thoughts of her past swarmed her mind. She wasn't a stranger to getting stood up by people she cared about. Working and keeping her hands busy tended to keep her mind off the negative thoughts and experiences from her past.

"Wait. *He?* You mean…" Jamie's mouth slowly opened.

"No, I don't mean, so stop gawking." Arianna chuckled, shaking her head. "He's just a random customer I met yesterday who also happens to be an amazing chef."

Jamie gasped. "Wait, he's not that celebrity chef everyone keeps talking about, is he?"

"He's not a celebrity as far as I know. Just a guy who knows how to treat your taste buds with the most amazing stuffed pimientos and cranberry sponge pudding, for starters."

"I heard some people talking about the guy making a huge, luxurious breakfast spread this morning."

"This morning?" Arianna frowned as she began stirring the batter for strawberry cake pops. *That couldn't really be Mark, could it?* After all, he'd promised to help her. "I don't see anything special about a bunch of bacon and eggs."

"I doubt it was just bacon and eggs he'd prepared." Jamie smiled coyly. "Either way, he's the talk of the town. And if he is, in fact, going to be working here alongside you, get ready for this place to be overwhelmed."

Arianna cringed. "Don't say that."

Jamie sighed dreamily. "You know, I think you two would make a great team. And you do need help around here. What better person to employ than that handsome chef?"

"You've seen him?"

"Who hasn't? If you weren't always cooped up in here, you might see some interesting things out in the world."

Arianna playfully stuck out her tongue. "Hey, I have a business to run. Bills to pay." But a thought lingered in her mind, and she wondered how many more women were attracted to his "celebrity chef" status. He seemed like a man with a big heart. But it was ridiculous to think that he would try to entertain everyone in town. Or was it? Arianna swallowed a lump in her throat. *Maybe I was just one of many on his list.*

"These customers won't lose their sweet tooth just because you decide to have a little break. Besides, it's almost Christmas, and you, the hardest-working person I know, don't deserve to spend it alone."

Arianna kept her eyes on the smooth batter as she added a cup of strawberry puree to it. She couldn't think of not working, especially during the holidays. Too many people were depending on her to make them smile. "I'll think about it," she finally told her friend.

Jamie clapped her hands together. "Great! I'm holding you to that, y'know. You better plan something before Christmas, or I'll plan it for you." She headed for the door. "Time to get back to it. Merry Christmas."

As soon as Jamie left, Arianna exhaled a deep sigh. She didn't want to believe that Mark had decided to break his promise. Didn't want to believe that helping at the bed-and-breakfast was more important than helping her. But how could she be upset at that? He was helping others, just as she would have done. Then again, she'd thought the same thing about Carson, her ex. Frowning, Arianna locked the front door once more. She had only three hours left to prepare, and she still had a lot more work to do.

As she turned to head around the counter, another knock came at the door. She started and looked over her shoulder. Mark stood beyond the powdered glass, clad in a leather jacket and red scarf.

Arianna's breath hitched. *Mark.* A mix of emotions swarmed her heart. She hesitated then went to the door and unlocked it. "Hey!" Her voice sounded more enthused than she'd intended.

Mark smiled apologetically. "Hey, sorry I'm late. One of the kitchen staff was trying to recreate the raisin bread I made for breakfast the other morning and ended up starting a fire in the kitchen when the bread burned so badly."

Arianna gasped. She felt two inches tall, remembering what she'd thought about him before. "Oh my goodness. Is everyone okay?"

"Everyone's fine." Mark nodded. "Paulette was a bit shaken up. Needless to say, she forbade Natalia, the kitchen staff member, to use the oven anymore. I felt bad for Natalia. She's fresh out of high school and wants to go to culinary school. She was just trying to help. Anyway, I helped her make the bread step by step, and it turned out great. Natalia was thrilled, nearly crying because she was so happy. There's hope for her yet."

Arianna stepped aside and let him in. As much as she wanted to scold Mark for breaking his promise to her, she couldn't bring herself to form the words. His selfless act was endearing, and it wasn't fair to be upset with him. "You seem to be in pretty high demand around here," she finally said.

"Blame Pauline." He rubbed the back of his head. "She's making me out to be some sort of celebrity."

"According to most of the town, you are."

"That's just crazy." He paused and sniffed. "Mmm. Something smells great."

"There are cookies and cupcakes in the oven, and I'm making cake pops. I'm a bit behind on where I need to be."

Mark pursed his lips. "That's my fault, and I'm sorry."

"No." She clenched her jaw. "I didn't mean for it to sound like that. I'm glad you saved the bed-and-breakfast from burning down."

"Still, I made you a promise."

She smiled at his insistence and decided not to argue about it. The sincere apology was one thing she would've never heard from her ex. He'd had no shame in hurting her. "Okay. We have two hours left to prepare before the shop officially opens."

Mark removed his jacket, revealing a brown knitted sweater underneath. He rolled up his sleeves and washed his hands in the kitchen sink. "So where do I start, boss?"

Arianna laughed, though the title had a nice ring to it. "Just Arianna's fine." She gestured to the pan of cooled tree-shaped cookies. "How about you start decorating those? Just paint them like festive Christmas trees like these." She pointed at a pan of extravagantly decorated tree cookies.

Mark nodded and approached the preparation counter. He picked up a squeeze bottle full of green icing and began carefully painting the trees.

Arianna noted his steady hand and extreme perfection as he coated the tree neatly and precisely in a matter of seconds. At this rate, they would finish all of the pastries in no time. She took a batch of cupcakes out of the oven then resumed making cake pops. She poured the batter into the cake pop maker and set it to Bake.

"I just noticed something," Mark suddenly said, not stopping his work. "This place isn't decorated for Christmas."

Arianna rolled her eyes. *Again?* "It is. You just didn't look hard enough."

Mark finished decorating three large cookies and moved on to the next three. He glanced over his shoulder at her. "A place like this deserves to be done up right. Especially with the amount of traffic you get through here."

"Eh, people care more about the treats than they do the interior decoration."

"It's all about atmosphere. And getting into the Christmas spirit."

"I haven't had time to decorate. Tonight's the Christmas parade, and I have to use every second to get these pastries done." She wasn't sure if her response was too harsh, but he had to understand that she was a businesswoman first and foremost. When he didn't reply, she turned her head, peering over her shoulder at him.

He'd already finished decorating an entire pan of cookies faster than she could blink. This guy ran circles around her when it came to productivity.

She prepared another large bowl of batter for a coconut cream cake. "So why in the world would Paulette the innkeeper think you're a celebrity?" she asked, trying to lighten the mood. "You didn't mention Justina's show, did you?"

"Of course not. She kept raving over that quiche I made and begged me to help make more breakfast items for the guests." Mark chuckled. "And I guess it didn't help that she knows I've worked in nice New

York restaurants. Apparently, my food's a hit now, and she's dubbed me a celebrity. Go figure."

"Paulette did come off as a bit… enthusiastic." Arianna fell silent as Mark stood next to her, holding a pan of cake pops. She sucked in a breath.

"How about I decorate these cake pops as little snowmen heads?" he suggested.

She considered it a moment then smiled. "Snowmen heads. I like it. It'll be a hit with the kids." Her heart warmed from his closeness. They shared something special in the kitchen, and they certainly made a great team when it came to efficiency.

Soon all of the pastries were baked, decorated, and placed in the display cases, ready for eager customers. The white hot chocolate was prepared and ready. They managed to beat the odds and finish forty-five minutes before noon.

Arianna slumped down in a chair and sighed, grateful that Mark had come in time to help. She hoped all of their hard work would pay off.

"So, about those decorations," Mark said, breaking her out of her thoughts.

Arianna looked at him curiously. "You want to decorate now? The shop will be opening soon."

Mark gave a dismissive wave. "Trust me. If we work together, in a half hour, we can turn this place into a Christmas paradise."

She thought about the Christmas decorations in the storage room. It would take forever to sort through everything. She slowly pointed at the storage room door beyond the kitchen.

Grinning, Mark flung open the door and hefted out a large bin that was overflowing with multicolored lights and silver garland. He set the bin in the middle of the floor at the front of the shop.

Arianna rummaged through the bin and pulled out two faux-fir wreaths. "I'll hang these up."

Mark nodded. "I'll get these lights untangled."

They worked quickly, unloading all of the decorations and putting each piece in place. In no time, the two of them had transformed the shop's interior into one with a memorable Christmas atmosphere. White lights hung from the ceiling, giving the illusion of tiny shining stars. Garland traced the window trim, and small Christmas knickknacks were placed strategically around the shop.

Arianna beamed proudly at their combined efforts.

"We make a great team." Mark glanced around admiringly.

She nodded. They certainly did, but in the back of her mind, she knew this teamwork would be short-lived, and in two days, he would be gone forever.

CHAPTER 5

MARK WAS AWAKE BEFORE SUNUP THE NEXT morning. He decided to try to sneak out of the house before Paulette or the other staff could nab him for breakfast again. While he found it flattering that they treated him like some celebrity, he also found it unnecessary and would rather spend time cooking alongside Arianna, who continued to capture his curious heart. Last night at her shop had been a great success. Despite the large crowds from the Christmas parade, Arianna ended up having enough product to sell and even had a few cookies left over, which she and Mark had shared as a victory celebration for their successful teamwork.

Bundled in his leather jacket and gloves, Mark crept out of his room and padded down the carpeted stairs. The place was unusually quiet. The scent of last night's flavorful cinnamon nut bread dessert lingered, reminding him of the small event Paulette had hosted when he returned from Arianna's shop. He made a beeline for the front door.

"Well, if it isn't the resident celebrity chef. Good morning to you!"

Mark rested his hand on the knob and froze. He looked toward the source of the voice, Richie Lawton, a mystery-author-in-residence. The older, balding man sat in a high-backed chair in the common room, his feet propped on an ottoman and a laptop computer in his lap. He tilted his head slightly, peering above the rim of his tortoiseshell glasses at Mark, and grinned.

Mark groaned inwardly. He regretted being late for work with Arianna yesterday, and he'd promised her it wouldn't happen again. "Good morning, Mr. Lawton." He plastered on a smile.

"Where might you be off to this early? I was hoping to get your opinion on a scene I've been working on. I was thinking that the chef's accomplice should be the victim's ex-wife. Wanna hear how it goes down?"

Mark winced. "I'd love to, sir, but I have a prior engagement."

Richie nestled back in his chair and refocused on the computer screen. "All right. Later then, eh? I need to do a bit of editing, anyway."

Turning back to the door, Mark exhaled a sigh of relief. Footsteps suddenly clopped along the wood floor, and his breath hitched.

"Oh, Mark! Thank goodness I caught you in time," Paulette's cheery voice called from the doorway leading to the dining room.

Mark deflated, slumping his shoulders. He spun around, facing the smiling older woman who shuffled over to him. "Good morning. Didn't expect to see you this early."

Paulette chuckled. "Oh, dearie, I'm always up before the sun. Gotta get the place ready for new visitors, you know." She stopped before him, clasping her hands together. "Today's Christmas Eve, which means the Christmas dessert contest is happening tonight at the square. I wanted to get your opinion on a gingerbread recipe."

Mark resisted the urge to roll his eyes. "Getting an opinion" usually involved him slaving over a hot stove. But he was reminded that Paulette had allowed him to stay here for free, thanks to his saving the bed-and-breakfast from burning down during Natalia's kitchen disaster. It was the very least he could do. "What kind of opinion do you need?"

"An honest one." Paulette took Mark's hand and led him to the kitchen. His senses were suddenly smacked with the scent of ginger. A pan of six gingerbread men sat on the counter.

He blinked. "Oh, you already made them."

"Of course I did, sweetie." Paulette laughed then took a cookie from the pan and gave it to him. "Have a taste and let me know what you think."

Mark hesitated then took the cookie. "I haven't even had breakfast yet."

"Yes, I know. That means your palate will be fresh so you can really give me an honest opinion. And don't worry. I whipped up a quick breakfast for you as thanks for all your help."

He let out a quiet sigh, part of him relieved that for once, he wouldn't be stuck in the kitchen again, but he still worried about losing precious time. He took a small bite. The cookie was flavorful and sweet, but something seemed to be missing. "Hmm..."

Paulette's smile faded. "You don't like it?"

"Oh, it's good, but I think you can draw more of the flavor out with a bit of orange zest." He stopped himself. *Uh-oh. What am I doing?*

Paulette's face lit up. "That sounds interesting. Never thought to use orange zest. Why don't you help me make a new batch?"

Mark's head spun. He opened his mouth to protest as she searched the refrigerator and fruit bowls.

"Gosh, I'm out of oranges," she continued, returning to him.

"The zest would taste best from navel oranges," Mark explained. "You'll get the best flavor from ones that are firm, weighty, and have a vibrant, consistent color." He stopped himself again. He couldn't help his eager-teacher side from showing up unannounced.

"Would you be a dear and get some from the store while you're out? Don't worry. I promise the next meal is on me, and I'll pay you for your time and troubles."

"I'd love to, but I promised Arianna I would help her at her shop this morning," Mark said.

Paulette gave him an innocent look. "I would never want to hold you up from meeting that girl you fancy, but this is a quick job. Besides, you know exactly what to get, and I wouldn't trust anyone else to do this. Especially not Natalia." She frowned.

Mark opened his mouth again then closed it. Paulette knew just what strings to pull. He was a sucker for helping anyone in the kitchen, and this was no exception. If he hurried, perhaps he would make it back in time to Arianna's shop. "All right. I'll get some."

"Excellent! There's a produce market one block over." Paulette plucked a cookie from the sheet and wrapped it in fresh cheesecloth. "Here, take this with you in case you decide something else is needed in the recipe."

He took the cheesecloth. "Thanks. You don't have to do all this."

"Oh, but I insist." She went to the stove and turned on the burners then retrieved the breakfast ingredients from the refrigerator and pantries. "Now, run along."

She didn't have to ask him twice, because he was already out the door in a flash.

It's been an hour, and he's still not here. Arianna scrambled to the oven to retrieve a pan of sugar cookies. She set them on the cooling rack and placed another batch in. She pulled out a pan of cooled cupcakes and dipped the tops in a white, sugary glaze then decorated them with blue fondant snowflakes. This was the second time in a row that Mark was late in helping her get the shop in order, and she realized she could no longer count on him. Despite his amazing culinary skills, he was unreliable. Definitely bad for business. And relationship material? Totally out of the question. She frowned as she cut out another snowflake from the fondant and placed it carefully on a glazed chocolate cupcake.

A knock came at the front door. Arianna paused and looked up. She met Mark's gaze, and he gave a small wave. Sighing, she finished decorating the cupcake and answered the door.

Mark looked at her apologetically, his lips forming a thin line. "Sorry. Got held up again."

Arianna's response was on the tip of her tongue. She wanted to tell him that she had everything under control. But the sad expression in his eyes gave her pause. She'd enjoyed the time they spent together yesterday, baking treats and decorating the shop. But Mark seemed stretched thin with an agenda of his own. Her heart stung. She was through living in the past. "It's all right," she finally said in a slightly choked voice.

"It's not all right," Mark said. "I promised you I would be here to help you as a temporary employee, and I've been late twice. I'll understand if you want to fire me."

Firing him was a tempting option. His constant tardiness would have been bad for any business, but his skills were invaluable. She'd never met anyone as attuned to detail in the kitchen. She wished she could make this work without constantly being reminded of her past. What a dilemma. Sighing, she finally shook her head. "No, I won't do that. You're just volunteering your time, anyway. I...I can't be upset that you have other obligations. I've got things taken care of."

He swallowed and looked toward the back counters, where scores of filled baking pans sat in the cooling racks. "You're finished already?"

"Just about." *No thanks to you.* She returned behind the counter and began setting the decorated cupcakes in the display case.

Mark deflated then slowly followed, carrying something small wrapped in a holly-printed cloth. He stood in front of the counter and watched her a moment. "I swear, I would've been here sooner, but Paulette wanted me to help her with her gingerbread cookie recipe. I had to get some oranges, but the nearby store wasn't open yet, so I tried the famer's market in the square, but I couldn't find the right type of navel oranges, and—" He paused and took a breath.

"Don't worry about it," she said, his poor apology doing little to ease the pain in her heart from his broken promise. "Honestly, I think I'll be better off just working alone like I have been already."

His mouth opened slightly.

"You clearly have other obligations with Paulette, and I don't want to stop you from that. It's fine, really. I'll manage."

"No," he whispered, hanging his head. "Give me another chance. Please. I promise not to do this again."

She regarded him skeptically. "How much weight does that promise really hold?"

"A lot. I want this to work."

"It's not going to work."

He slumped his shoulders and averted his gaze. Arianna could sense his genuine disappointment. Perhaps he had learned his lesson. She could only hope. "Third time's a charm," as the saying went.

"Okay, I'll give you one last chance. If you're late again, you can just find yourself another pastry shop to volunteer your time at." It pained her to say such words, and she saw the hurt in his eyes, but she was tired of hurting, too. She had to break this cycle.

Mark's head lifted, a smile returning to his lips. "Absolutely. I promise. Thank you." He set the cloth on the counter, revealing a perfectly shaped and classically decorated gingerbread man. "Paulette made this."

Arianna glanced at the cookie and was reminded of the Christmas dessert contest. She couldn't believe it was Christmas Eve already. The dessert contest was her favorite event, and every year, she entered.

Though she had yet to win, that hadn't stopped her from entering. The competition encouraged her to attempt new recipes as well as get new ideas. This year, she'd been so caught up in her business that she hadn't had time to think of the perfect dessert to whip up. "For the contest? I'm not surprised. Paulette enters every year."

"She's a great cook and all, but you're way better."

Arianna snorted. "You're just being nice. I've gone up against her only once with a fruitcake recipe. She smoked me with her rich and creamy peppermint pie recipe." She cringed at the terribly low scores she'd received from the judges' panel.

"Desserts are your specialty," Mark said. "You deserve to win. Maybe you just had a bad panel of judges."

Arianna turned, pulled out a pan of cooled cookies from the rack, and began adding them to the display case. "Nope. All of them are local food connoisseurs who frequent all the eateries, cafés, and bakeries around town. According to the judges, my cake wasn't moist enough, and I used a little too much cinnamon."

Mark went around the counter. "Let me help you with those." He pulled off his gloves, threw off his jacket, and washed his hands in the small hand sink in the back room.

When he returned, Arianna pursed her lips and pulled out another pan of finished cookies from the rack. "That… that's not necessary. Why don't you help Paulette?"

He looked at her with slight annoyance in his eyes. "I've helped Paulette enough. Now I want to help you. Starting with these cookies."

She frowned. "Fine. They go in there." She nodded toward the adjacent display case.

He got to work. She returned to the decorating counter and prepared some fondant to decorate the batch of cake pops.

"You do still want to enter the contest, right?" Mark asked, breaking the brief silence.

Arianna thought about it. Entering the contest always did wonders for her business. She usually expected to see the entire town crowd into her shop, wanting to have a taste of her entry. This year, however, she wasn't sure what to enter, nor did she think she had enough time to make something before tonight. She shrugged at Mark. "I don't know."

"Oh, c'mon. You're an amazing pastry chef. And your customers obviously make that loud and clear. It's time you tried something new and exciting and maybe offer it as a seasonal treat. That would be a hit."

So many great ideas. Arianna sighed. *Do I really have a chance of beating Paulette this time?* With Mark staying at her bed-and-breakfast, Paulette had an ace up her sleeve. Then again, so did Arianna. "Well…"

Mark's smile grew. "I'll even help you find a good recipe. Something that no one would ever think of. That's really the key to winning these types of contests."

She looked at him again, the corner of her lips tugging upward. "Oh, all right. I'll give it a try. But what recipe should we make?"

Mark thought for a moment then snapped his fingers. "I got it. Plum pudding cake pops."

Her brow furrowed. "What?"

He nodded. "It's a spin on a tasty, classic Christmas dessert. You're great at making cake pops, and I've been dying to make plum pudding again, so we'll combine talents and make something unique that will stand out above all the other entries."

"What makes you think no one else will try that? A lot of people enter this competition every year."

"Even if someone else makes plum pudding cake pops, they won't taste as good as ours."

She couldn't help smiling at that. Mark's cranberry sponge pudding was divine. She had no doubt the plum pudding would be just as tasty. And her cake pops were indeed a hit, always the first to sell out. Perhaps combining their talents would give them a competitive advantage. "All right. Let's do it."

They worked quickly until noon. Mark prepared the pudding, while Arianna created the cake. She was delighted to work alongside him, creating something new and exciting. They seemed to have perfect chemistry in the kitchen. *If only he was more reliable...*

While the pudding steamed on the stove, they cleaned up and opened the shop for the afternoon rush. A woman and her daughter were the first ones at the counter.

"Merry Christmas! How may I help you?" Arianna smiled brightly.

"Merry Christmas," the woman replied. "I would like one of your Christmas Memories pairings, please."

"Coming right up." Arianna eyed Mark, who gave her a thumbs-up. He used metal tongs to pluck a Christmas stocking cookie from a pan in the display case. Then he placed it in a small box.

"It's great to see you have help for a change, Arianna," the woman said, handing her some money.

"Yes, he's been wonderful. I couldn't ask for a better helper." Arianna chuckled.

"Oh, Mommy! This is so good!"

Arianna and the woman looked at the little girl, who held a gingerbread man. A tiny chunk of its head was gone.

The woman gasped and took the cookie from her. "Jenny! Where did you get this?"

The little girl frowned and pointed at the folded cloth on the counter.

"I'm sorry. I totally did not see that there," Arianna told the woman.

Mark sighed. "Ugh. My fault. I forgot to pick that up."

The woman's surprised look bounced from Mark to Arianna. "Was this made today?"

Arianna opened her mouth then closed it.

"Around six this morning," Mark answered with a nod.

"You know," the woman said, "Jenny dislikes the taste of gingerbread. But she absolutely loves this. Now I have to try this for myself."

"But—" Arianna raised her hand to the woman, but she wasn't able to stop her from nibbling a piece of the cookie.

The woman's face lit up brighter than the Christmas lights. "This is incredible! How much are these?"

Arianna sighed. "I'm sorry, but they're not for sale. My gingerbread cookies look like these." She pointed at the heavily decorated tree-shaped and snowman-shaped gingerbread cookies in the display case.

"That cookie was made by Paulette of White Pine Bed & Breakfast," Mark explained. "But if you like that, then you'll love Arianna's cookies much more."

The woman shook her head and gave the rest of the cookie to her daughter. "Oh, Paulette. I adore her. I don't think any cookie would be better than this. I do hope she enters them in the dessert contest because she certainly has my vote!"

Arianna cringed. She was starting to have second thoughts about entering that contest. She glanced at the stove, where the plum pudding continued to steam over one of the burners. As she watched the mother and daughter happily leave the shop, Arianna wondered how much Mark had helped with those cookies. Was it really his recipe? Or was he using her and Paulette to test recipes for his own personal gain? Then she had another disturbing thought: did Mark intend to enter both recipes in the contest at the same time?

CHAPTER 6

ARIANNA STARED AT THE CLOCK IN THE KITCHEN and sighed. Her time with Mark was short-lived when he'd suddenly had to leave a few hours earlier. Paulette had called him to help with a kitchen emergency caused by another one of her new kitchen staff members. Arianna couldn't very well keep him in her shop. He was volunteering, after all. But her heart still stung every time he had to leave. She didn't want to be selfish by assuming her problems were more relevant than Paulette's. Clearly, they weren't. Yet every time she felt happiness in her heart, it was suddenly ripped away, much like in her past relationships.

But Arianna didn't want to think about relationships. Besides, the rush had begun to die down the closer it got to time for the dessert contest. She stared at the plum pudding cake pops sitting on a large cake plate. While she figured the dessert wouldn't score many points in the Aesthetics category, she was confident it would earn points for Taste and Originality. And how would the cake pops fare against the gingerbread cookies that Mark and Paulette were entering?

Thoughts of Mark rushed to her mind again. Before he'd left to help Paulette, he'd promised Arianna that he would represent Sweet Peach Bake Shop as a team member. Was he about to break another promise?

With a sigh, Arianna rolled out batches of green and red fondant, carved some holly leaf and holly berry shapes, and began decorating the cake pops.

The front door opened, and hurried footsteps approached. Arianna looked up from her decorating.

Beaming wide, Jamie stood at the front counter and waved. "Hey, girl. The dessert contest's starting in less than an hour. You coming or what?"

Arianna chewed her bottom lip and stared at the tiny decorated pudding domes. "What do you think of these?"

Jamie furrowed her brow. "What are they?"

Arianna frowned. If Jamie didn't know what they were, then Arianna would probably have bad luck with the judges. "Don't you know plum pudding cake pops when you see them?"

Jamie perked up. "Oh, right! Not like I see those too often. Come to think of it, I don't think I've ever seen those."

"Yeah."

"They look more like chocolate cake pops than plum pudding ones. But hey, I'm just the emcee for the contest, not a judge."

Arianna deflated.

"What's wrong?"

Arianna filled her friend in about Mark and the cooking debacle. By the time she finished, Jamie's cheery expression was gone.

"I'm sorry to hear he's been flaking out on you like that," Jamie said. "I guess when you're a big-deal celebrity chef, you're in high demand."

"I just wish he wouldn't play around with my emotions like that. We work so well together. He helped me make all the shop treats as well as these cake pops."

Jamie shrugged. "He's not worth stressing over. Besides, you don't need him to make awesome stuff. You were doing great before he came along. If he's going to keep flaking out on you and leaving you high and dry, he's not worth stressing over."

Oof. That's harsh. Arianna felt as if all the wind had gotten knocked out of her. "Maybe you're right."

Jamie cracked a reassuring smile and patted Arianna's back. "Of course I'm right. But who knows? Maybe he'll finally come around and realize just how important you are. Though this contest is going to be interesting if he's entering two things he's made. I don't even think that's allowed."

"He's helping Paulette as thanks for her allowing him to stay at the bed-and-breakfast for free," Arianna explained. "He really has no reason to help me."

"He obviously wants to help you. Unfortunately, he won't be able to enter both."

"The judges won't know he's worked on both."

"True, but you and I do, and as a committee member, I must inform the others of this violation of the rules. He'll have to choose."

Arianna swallowed. *Which one will he choose?*

Thomas, one of the bed-and-breakfast's college-intern kitchen staff members, added a final dab of frosting to the last gingerbread man's shirt button. Mark watched him like a hawk. Mark had regretted leaving Arianna's shop early to help avert yet another kitchen disaster.

Making a grave error, Thomas had accidentally used wax paper instead of parchment paper to bake a batch of gingerbread cookies and had sparked an oven fire. Thankfully, Mark had managed to rush there in time to extinguish it before firefighters arrived. Thomas was visibly shaken by the ordeal, and Paulette gave the young man a stern talking to, threatening to fire him for his recklessness. But Mark, who had seen more than his share of kitchen disasters, decided this was the best time to teach the young chef about basic kitchen safety.

Thomas finished decorating the cookie and pulled back, admiring his work, then eyed Mark for confirmation.

Mark nodded and gave him a thumbs-up. In two hours, under Mark's close watch, Thomas helped Paulette bake two dozen gingerbread men. Despite Mark having to leave Arianna early, he was confident in the outcome of their plum pudding cake pops, thanks to his and Arianna's teamwork. Arianna was sure to win on originality and taste alone.

"Oh, you were right, Mark. The orange zest makes them taste absolutely perfect now!" Paulette raved after nibbling on a cookie sample. "I'm so glad you came here at just the right time." She glared at Thomas. "I'm banning you from the kitchen. I've already seen enough scares in less than a week."

Thomas hung his head. "I'm sorry. It won't happen again. Please, it was an honest mistake."

Paulette crossed her arms. "Do you realize how many people's lives you put in danger from your 'honest mistake'?"

Thomas sighed.

"Hey, give him a break, Paulette," Mark said. "He's still learning, just like I did. And believe me, I've caused far worse kitchen disasters than this."

Thomas widened his eyes. "You have?"

"Everyone just starting out has." Mark patted his back reassuringly then acknowledged Paulette. "You know, he has the makings of being a great chef someday. He's got steady hands, precision, creativity, and a drive to learn."

Thomas's face brightened. "Th-thank you, sir."

Paulette frowned. "I'll forgive you this time because it's Christmas. But be more careful next time. Understand?"

"Yes, ma'am. Absolutely!" Thomas straightened.

Paulette dismissed the young intern, and she and Mark were alone.

"These cookies are sheer winners in this year's contest. We make a great team."

"We?" Mark raised his eyebrows. Was Paulette considering entering him as her teammate? He didn't want to imagine what Arianna would think if that were to happen. "I can't take any credit for this," he said quickly. "The cookies were your idea. And Thomas did all the work."

"But these cookies wouldn't have turned out the way they have without your key suggestion," she countered.

"That's all it was—a suggestion. The real work was between you and Thomas. You should enter this as the bed-and-breakfast's team."

"Oh, I intend to, but you have singlehandedly turned this place around with your generosity. I think it's only fitting that you represent White Pine Bed & Breakfast as the resident celebrity chef."

Mark had opened his mouth to reply when his cell phone suddenly buzzed in his back pocket, startling him. He pulled out the phone, and a familiar number flashed on the screen. *Justina's studio*. His heart pounded. "I need to take this call," he told Paulette.

"Of course. I'll get these cookies all packed and ready to take down to the square."

Mark left the kitchen and went up to his room, climbing the stairs two at a time. "Hello?" He shut the door to his suite and leaned against it.

"Good evening, Mr. Ellison," came a chatty voice amid the continuous sounds of clacking keyboard keys. "This is Lizzy from Emerald 96 Studios. Do you have some time to chat?"

His heart beat faster. A call from the studio? At this hour? Then he remembered the time difference and realized it was only four o'clock in Las Vegas. "Uh, sure. How can I help you?"

"Justina fell ill last week, which forced us to do a little finagling with the schedules. Unfortunately, we'll have to rebook the winners' appearances on the show at a later date, due to a prior commitment to Bruce Tanaka. No hard feelings, Mark, but well…"

"Bruce is a world-famous chef. I get it," Mark finished. While it was heartbreaking to find out he wouldn't be on Justina's show as planned, he couldn't be more honored to think that he would be replaced by another of his idols, one of the most prominent celebrity chefs in the world.

"We're still really looking forward to having you on the show," Lizzie insisted. "However, things like this happen often, and we have to adapt to these changes. If you would still like to appear on the show, I'll need your confirmation of the schedule change. If a later date doesn't work for you, then I can see what I can do about squeezing you into the filler portion of one of our end segments."

Mark made a face. *Fly all the way out there for a three-minute segment?* But even in those three minutes, he would be able to spend priceless moments with Justina, his idol, and be exposed to national marketing, which would be valuable for his career. *That alone would be worth the trip, right?*

"How 'bout it, Mr. Ellison?" Lizzie asked again after some moments of silence.

Mark gritted his teeth. If he flew to Vegas, he would be free from Paulette, but he would also be apart from Arianna. Something about the eager young pastry chef intrigued him. In the few days since he'd met her, she'd practically stolen his heart. He deflated, his shoulders slouching. "I… I don't know…."

The insistent typing suddenly stopped. "I'll need an answer today, Mr. Ellison. But I will tell you this. Opportunities like these don't come often, especially where Justina is concerned. With her popularity, it's extremely difficult to book an exclusive spot with her like this."

Mark swallowed. His career as a world-famous chef rested on his decision.

"What's it going to be, Mr. Ellison?"

CHAPTER 7

THIS WAS A BAD IDEA. ARIANNA STARED AT THE twenty-two other contestants. They stood behind their delicious-looking dessert entries sitting on six-foot tables lining the crowded town square. She frowned at her drab plate of plum pudding cake pops. Not even the fondant holly berries she'd added had increased the aesthetic appeal, compared to some of the other entries of heavily decorated Christmas cookies, brownies, and fruitcakes.

A woman next to her—Cassie White, owner of the small clothing boutique a few blocks down from the sweet shop—stood proudly with her creative display of Christmas tree–shaped linzer torte cookies. Cassie side-eyed Arianna then the cake pops. Her eyebrow slowly arched.

Arianna pursed her lips, turned away from the woman's assessing gaze, and focused on the group of four judges, who began visiting each table, sampling the entries. The crowd watched and cheered for the entrants. Jamie walked ahead of the judges, stopping at each table to write down the contestants' names. Arianna scanned the contestants again and realized that one of the six-foot tables was empty. She furrowed her brow. She hadn't seen Mark or Paulette. Could they have forfeited the contest? Arianna frowned. Mark had spoken loud and clear. He couldn't keep promises, and Christmas was the worst time to deal with this kind of disappointment. She would rather have stayed at her shop instead of standing here awaiting public humiliation. *How could I have trusted him to be here for me when he keeps flaking out like this?*

"Hey, girl! So good to see you!"

Arianna stared at Jamie, who had walked ahead of the judges still crowded around the first table. She clutched her clipboard. "Hey..."

Jamie's bright smile faltered. "What's wrong? It's not like you to be so glum during a dessert contest."

Arianna sighed. "After seeing all these other wonderful entries, I don't think I'll stand a chance."

Jamie acknowledged the cake pops then tilted her head. "I bet you'll get points for uniqueness, at least."

"Thanks for trying to cheer me up."

"What about your new employee? Mark, wasn't it?" Jamie looked around curiously.

Arianna's frown deepened. "Don't remind me. I…" She paused, noticing movement out of the corner of her eye. The empty table from earlier was now occupied by Paulette, the bed-and-breakfast owner, and a young helper. The old woman set down a plate of gingerbread cookies and stood behind her table.

Odd. Where's Mark?

Jamie's eyes suddenly went wide. "Oh—"

"Huh?" A gentle hand touched Arianna's shoulder. She jumped, spun around, and widened her eyes. "Mark!"

Mark scowled. "Sorry I'm late. I owe you a huge explanation."

Her mind was a jumble of emotions. She was torn between trying to understand his broken promises and her disappointed heart.

"Hey there." Jamie gave a small wave. "So I have some bad news. It has come to my attention that you submitted multiple dessert entries, so I'll have to disqualify one."

Mark's eyes widened. "What? That's impossible. I only helped Arianna."

"Well, apparently…"

Arianna chewed her bottom lip.

Mark looked at Arianna, his eyes full of hurt. "Is this true? Did you tell her I submitted multiple entries?"

Her heart pounded. "I'd assumed you helped make those gingerbread man cookies with Paulette."

Mark's jaw clenched. "That's not true. I supervised the baking process to make sure there were no more kitchen disasters, but that was all. Paulette and her intern chef, Thomas, did all the work."

If Arianna felt any smaller, she would disappear. What sort of apology could she come up with to smooth over this huge misunderstanding? How could she be upset with him for helping others? *How selfish am I?*

"Oh, that's great news!" Jamie beamed. "Because I would've hated to disqualify any delicious dessert. So, I should put you two down as a team?"

Arianna stayed silent. Frustration, anger, and sadness swarmed her mind. She would understand if Mark didn't want to be on her team after such a terrible accusation.

"Yes, put us down as Team Sweet Peach," Mark told Jamie with a curt nod.

Arianna gawked at him.

"Excellent!" Jamie scribbled on her clipboard. "Good luck, you two!"

After Jamie moved on to the next contestant, Arianna turned to Mark. "You still want to be on my team?"

Mark appeared taken aback. "Of course I do. We made those cake pops together, after all."

"Yes, but after what I said… I'm… I'm sorry."

He shook his head. "Don't apologize. I understand why you were concerned, especially when I haven't been good about keeping promises. I'll admit, I've stretched myself thin, trying to make people happy. Anyway, those cookies were all Paulette's and Thomas's efforts, not mine. I'm just a guest at her bed-and-breakfast, and I'm not beholden to her, even though I did help her with some of the meals."

Arianna breathed a sigh of relief. "I'm sorry for doubting you."

Mark gently took her hand in his. "I'm sorry, too. I've been a horrible employee."

Arianna looked at their clasped hands, and she smiled softly. "You are a great man with a big heart. I can never be upset about that."

He gazed into her eyes with care and concern. Arianna gave his hand a small, reassuring squeeze.

The four judges walked up to their table and stared as if intrigued at the plate of cake pops. "And what do we have here?" one of the judges asked.

Arianna quickly released Mark's hand and addressed the redheaded judge, who wore a badge that read, "Eric, columnist, *The Traveling Chef*."

"Hello. I would like to present to you our fabulous plum pudding cake pops."

"Now there's something you don't see every day," another judge said. Her badge read, "Sandra, food critic, *Cooks & Travel*." Her emerald-green eyes focused briefly on the clipboard in her pale, slender hands.

"That's right." Mark spoke up. "We wanted to do something a little different than the norm."

"Plum pudding is such a staple Christmas dessert," another judge said. His badge read, "Jake, head chef, Frandles Restaurant." The portly middle-aged man was of average height and wore a stern expression on his pockmarked face. "At least, it once was back in the old days. It's a shame you don't see it as often as you used to."

"They're not exactly aesthetically pleasing, for one," another judge said. Her badge read, "Brenda, owner, Cute & Tasty Sweet Shop." The young woman's full rosy-red lips twisted into a smirk.

Arianna frowned. Brenda's shop was all the way on the other side of town, so they weren't exactly competitors. "No, they really aren't," Arianna agreed, "but looks can be deceiving." She handed each of the judges a cake pop.

The judges took a small bite. Arianna chewed her bottom lip as she watched their faces carefully.

"This is surprisingly good!" Sandra's face lit up. "I think I need another bite." She ended up eating the rest of her cake pop.

"You know, plum pudding can be hard to master, due to its nature and the fact that it's such an old recipe," Eric said. "But you've managed to capture the very essence of this pudding perfectly. Not too much nutmeg, the texture is on point, and the cake is very moist."

Arianna exchanged a grin with Mark.

"I would've liked to have seen it made a little more festive looking," Brenda said.

"I think it's fine." Jake waved his hand dismissively. "It's made the way it's intended. I, for one, appreciate the simple classic appeal."

Arianna sucked in her breath as she watched the judges scribble their scores on their clipboards. An event volunteer who was following the judges presented them a palate-cleansing plate of apple slices. The judges plucked a slice from the plate and moved on to the next contestant—Cassie.

Arianna exhaled. Her heart still pounded. "You think we stand a chance?" she whispered to Mark.

Mark gave her a thumbs-up. "I think we impressed the judges enough to give us a chance."

"I dunno. They seemed pretty hung up on the physical appearance."

"As you said, appearances can be deceiving."

Arianna grinned, admiring his optimism. She looked over at Cassie's table, where the judges wore mixed expressions as they tasted her linzer torte cookies. Finally, several contestants later, the judges stopped in front of Paulette's table, where she and a younger man stood. The judges sampled her gingerbread man cookies. All of the judges wore awe-inspired expressions and wide grins as they remained at her table much longer than they stayed with previous contestants.

She must've captivated the judges with her cookies so much they don't want to leave. Arianna leaned over to Mark and whispered, "What do you think they're talking to Paulette about?"

Frowning, he didn't take his eyes off them. "I don't know."

"They really like her cookies."

"Yeah, I figured they would."

After several more moments, the judges finally moved on to the next contestant. Paulette's face was flushed with her obvious excitement.

Fifteen more agonizing minutes passed as the judges finished sampling the final contestant's entry. They turned in their clipboards to Jamie, who tallied the scores. She stepped up to the podium in the middle of the square and addressed the crowd. "Ladies and gentlemen! I am pleased to announce this year's runner-up and winner for the annual White Pine Christmas Dessert Contest! We've had a variety of amazing Christmas desserts this time around, and the judges were wholly impressed with all of them. The judges' scores were based on four key factors: taste, originality, theme, and aesthetics.

"But first, I would like to ask that our final two contestants please join me at the podium. Our first finalist is Paulette Jones, representing White Pine Bed & Breakfast, and featuring her fabulous gingerbread man cookies!"

The crowd went wild with cheers and victory shouts. Paulette's face lit up as if she were surprised, and she and her young helper hurried to the podium.

Arianna exhaled a breath. *Of course she made runner-up. She'll probably win, too.* She crossed her arms, waiting for the next finalist to be called.

"Our second finalist is…" Jamie grinned. "Arianna Willis, representing Team Sweet Peach of Sweet Peach Bakery!"

Another wave of whistles and applause swept through the crowd. Arianna's heart stopped a moment. *Me? I'm a finalist? Did I hear that correctly?* It wasn't until she noticed Mark's beaming face that she realized it was true. She hustled to the podium with Mark on her heels. They stood on one side of Jamie while Paulette and her assistant stood on the other. Paulette leaned over, meeting Arianna's gaze, and smiled.

Arianna tried to smile back, but she'd suspected the woman already knew her win was guaranteed. There was no way Arianna's plum pudding cake pops would be able to stand up to Paulette's seemingly flawless gingerbread cookies. She regarded Mark worriedly. Mark remained focused on Jamie, but Arianna noticed a hint of doubt and fear in his eyes. Maybe these plum pudding cake pops were too different for this crowd, compared to the tried-and-true traditional gingerbread cookies. Arianna reached for Mark's hand again, her fingers gently touching his. His gaze faltered, and he looked at her for a moment then cracked a small smile.

Jamie acknowledged everyone at the podium. "It was a tough decision from the judges, and it came down to the wire. There were a lot of amazing entries this year. But now, it's time to announce the winner for this year's Christmas bake-off!" She took Arianna and Paulette's hands and led them to the front of the podium. "The competition was stiff this year. There was a one-point difference between the winner and runner-up. So I am pleased to announce the winner, with a combined score of a *perfect* twenty for taste, nineteen for originality, seventeen for theme, and nine for aesthetics, and an overall score of sixty-five points is..." She raised Arianna's arm. "Arianna Willis of Team Sweet Peach!"

For a moment, Arianna felt the world around her grow smaller. Her ears rang. She wasn't sure if what she was hearing was actually happening or if it was just some hopeful thought. Then she heard the crowd roaring in victory and the distinct chants of "Sweet Peach" amid the shouts and claps.

Mark squeezed her hand. "We did it!"

"We..." Arianna stared in disbelief at Mark's excited face.

We did it!

 Chapter 8

MARK PACKED HIS SUITCASE AND ROLLED IT TO the front door of his suite. He took one last look at the charming, cozy room, which was decorated nicely for the holidays. Tonight was a whirlwind of emotions. He'd been almost moved to tears when he gazed upon Arianna's shocked face as her name was announced as the Christmas dessert contest winner. It was her first-ever win and well deserved. They made a great team, and Mark hoped that she would let him work alongside her again. They'd celebrated her victory in the square, though it was short-lived, as she was exhausted after a long, stressful day. He'd decided to walk her home afterward. Arianna didn't bother saying goodbye, with not even a hug or a good night kiss. Perhaps, he had thought, she was still so overwhelmed with emotions that simple goodbyes hadn't crossed her mind.

Mark had understood and respected her decision. Tonight was her night. But a small part of him had hoped they would make their celebration a little more romantic. Perhaps she was still unsure of him.

But the time had ended for finding out if their relationship could work. Mark thought it best to check out of White Pine Bed & Breakfast. The disappointed expression on Paulette's face hadn't gone unnoticed. She'd treated him like royalty during his stay, and in the end, he'd betrayed her trust. She'd left the square quickly before Mark had a chance to talk to her. He'd figured she was upset, and she'd had every right to be. How was he going to explain himself this time?

He left his suite and carried his suitcase down the narrow wooden stairs. White Christmas lights wrapped around the bannister provided a glowing path as he descended. Entering the common room, he discovered Richie seated in his usual spot, his gaze tuned to his laptop screen. Mark pursed his lips and quietly padded toward the kitchen, hoping to find Paulette there.

"Checking out tonight?" Richie asked.

Mark froze and looked over his shoulder. "Yeah, I think I'm going to stay at a motel in town or something."

"You'd rather leave a place like this on Christmas Eve?"

"Yeah, well. Things don't always go as planned."

"I know how that is." Richie gave a small salute. "Have a safe trip back home, and Merry Christmas."

"Merry Christmas." Mark saluted back. He turned around and discovered Paulette standing in the doorway. He flinched. "Hey, I was just looking for you."

"Mm-hmm." She regarded him and his luggage sadly. Then she walked into the kitchen.

Mark's throat tightened. He followed her while he attempted to fish for the right words to say. As he entered the kitchen, he noticed the shining silver runner-up plaque affixed prominently to the cream-colored wall. "Uh, I know it's a bit awkward with me leaving like this, but… unfortunately, a… business deal went bust, so I need to head back home."

Paulette's lips formed a thin line.

Mark felt his heart pound faster. *Geez, she must be furious with me.* "I'm sorry about everything that happened. But I just want to say I'm eternally grateful for your hospitality. I know you allowed me to stay here for free and all, but I insist on paying you what I owe. It's only fair, especially after what happened tonight."

A small wrinkle formed at her brow. "What are you going on about?"

Mark blinked. "Didn't you hear anything I said?"

"I heard you, and it's nonsense. You will not pay me a cent after all the amazing things you've done for me and my business."

It was Mark's turn to look confused. "What are you talking about? I'm not a celebrity chef."

"Of course you are." Paulette gave a dismissive wave.

"I messed up your chances of winning that contest by helping Arianna."

A small smile grew on Paulette's lips. "You didn't mess anything up. If anything, you made things better. Even though I didn't win, just the recognition of being a runner-up has done wonders for my business. This place is already booked solid for next week! And the calls keep coming in. All thanks to your charming suggestion of adding orange zest to those cookies. You've done more than I could ever ask."

"Then why are you upset?"

"I'm upset because you're leaving me. And on Christmas Eve to boot. How can you do such a thing?"

Mark swallowed. "I thought you might not want me around after what happened today."

Paulette shook her head. "I can't be upset with you saving my business from burning down, mentoring my young employees, and bringing so much positive exposure to this place."

Mark opened his mouth to retort then closed it. *Did I really do all this?*

"By the way," Paulette continued in a coy tone, "I already knew that you fancied that charming young pastry chef. Arianna is a special shining star who loves making people smile. You two have a lot in common in that respect. Why would I ever want to stop you from being with her? You both did something amazing tonight."

Mark exhaled a breath he had been inadvertently holding. "Thanks for understanding."

"Of course. Now go put that suitcase back. You don't need to be traveling on Christmas Eve. You at least need to stay until tomorrow. I'm planning the biggest holiday get-together."

"But wouldn't you want to use that suite for actual paying customers?"

She shook her head. "Right now, I want that room to be occupied by our current resident celebrity chef. Now put that suitcase back and go see Arianna." She pointed at the stairs.

Mark grinned and left the kitchen.

Arianna adjusted the shiny gold winner's plaque hanging prominently on the wall behind the front counter of her shop. She stood back and admired the plaque, still in awe that all of this was real. In all the years she'd been a professional pastry chef, she'd never won an award for her efforts. After the contest was over, she was interviewed by the local news station. Her mind was a jumble of thoughts as she stood before the news anchor, answering his brief questions. She'd wished Mark had joined her, but he'd insisted she have her moment of glory to help boost her business.

After her interview, people approached her, asking when she would have the plum pudding cake pops in stock. It looked like she would have yet another item on her holiday menu once the shop reopened after Christmas. For now, however, she decided to spend Christmas Eve enjoying the fruits of her and Mark's efforts.

Mark. Arianna sighed. She would never be able to understand that mysterious, charming chef who'd come into her life and, within a few days, turned it upside down. But they separated without so much as a hug or good night kiss, something she had hoped for to make the night truly magical. Perhaps it was for the best that they hadn't. She had no time for relationships, especially when her business would be extra busy soon.

A rapping noise came from the glass window on the front door. Startled, Arianna spun around. Her shop was closed until the day after Christmas, and she'd hoped the curious passerby would notice the sign.

She did a double take. Mark stood beyond the door, his hair and leather coat powdered with snow. Her heart fluttered. She rushed to the door, unlocked it, and flung it open. "You came back!"

Beaming, Mark shook off the snow and stepped inside. "I figured you'd still be here ogling that plaque. Which was well deserved, I might add. It looks good, by the way. No one can ever miss seeing that."

Her cheeks warmed. "I still can't believe it. I can't believe this actually happened."

"Well, believe it. You and your shop will be the talk of the town."

Her smile faded slightly. "You had just as much to do with it. The pudding was your idea, after all."

"You inspired that idea, so it was a combined effort."

Arianna laughed.

"Hey, I wanted to apologize again for flaking out on you and breaking my promises."

She opened her mouth, slightly surprised at that. "I will admit, I was hurt. I've been hurt before, and I didn't want to feel that again. But I didn't realize just how much you were spreading yourself thin, trying to help me and Paulette. I was selfish to think you didn't care. But you really are a good man who cares."

Mark's face softened. He stepped closer to her. "I care very much." He paused, his lips turning to a frown. "I have something to tell you."

She tilted her head curiously.

"I won't be going to Vegas for Justina's show."

"What? Why?"

He shook his head. "I thought about it for a long time. It's just not something I would enjoy, knowing I would be thousands of miles away from you."

Her cheeks went red. "Mark…"

"I'm leaving after Christmas, then I'll be headed back home to Long Island to look for a new job."

She chewed her bottom lip. He would be all the way in Long Island while she would be up here in White Pine. Long-distance relationships never tended to work. But she couldn't easily let him go either. "You know, Jake, the head chef at Frandles, was asking about you after the contest. He was hoping to talk to you about the open sous chef position."

Mark blinked. "Really?"

She nodded. "I figured you might be interested, but… it'd be kind of useless since you don't live here."

He pursed his lips. "Maybe I need to change that."

"What?"

"I'm not beholden to my apartment. I'd hoped the Vegas deal would be my big break. But after coming here, after meeting you, I'm glad it fell through."

Arianna was speechless.

He reached out and took her hand. "I'm going to move to White Pine. I like it here. The people are friendly, and I met the most adorable, kindhearted pastry chef."

She smiled and squeezed his hand. "Isn't that a bit of a drastic move, uprooting from the city life and coming here?"

"It is, in some ways. But I can already tell that living in White Pine will be a lot less stressful than the big-city life. It might be the change I need in my life, at least for now. I'll live here for a while and make a short-term commitment at Frandles and see how things go." He gently rubbed her hand. "And maybe it will give us time to see where things go, too."

Her smile broadened. His grand plan sounded promising. "I think I'd like that."

"Living here, being able to see you every day, would be the best Christmas present ever." He slowly drew his face closer to hers.

Arianna hesitated. *He'd give up his city life and live out here just to see me.* While she'd never had anyone so willing to sacrifice for her, it flattered her beyond anything she had ever known. She slowly drew forward and met his lips with a gentle, soft kiss. Then she released his hand and wrapped her arms around him. They indulged in a deep, passionate kiss that spread warmth and happiness to her heart.

Mark finally broke the kiss, but his face remained close to hers. "Paulette's having a big get-together at the bed-and-breakfast tomorrow for Christmas. She insisted that you come."

Arianna beamed then planted another kiss on his lips. "I wouldn't miss it for the world."

THE END

ABOUT THE AUTHOR

MARIE LONG is a novelist who enjoys the snowy weather, the mountains, and a cup of hot white chocolate. She's an avid supporter of literacy movements. To learn more about her, visit her website: www.marielongauthor.com.